let's look at

kitchen

Plates and things

Glasses, bowls and plates are often kept in the cupboard.

four
soup bowls

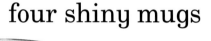

four shiny mugs

four dinner plates

four coloured
glasses

milk jug

fat teapot

water jug

vegetable dish

Let's put these
things away.

Dried foods

These foods can be
kept for a long time.

white
flour

kidney
beans

dried apricots

red lentils

white rice

pasta tubes

coffee beans

crunchy biscuits

leaf tea

Just one more biscuit, while Mum's not looking!

sun-dried raisins

long spaghetti

Tins, bottles and jars

Some food is put into special containers.

cherries in syrup

tuna fish

tomato ketchup

sticky apricot jam

golden apple juice

creamy tomato soup

olive oil

thick honey

sunflower oil

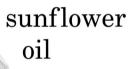

I'm having jam on my toast ...

crunchy peanut butter

... I hope!

In the fridge

Some food needs to be kept cold to stay fresh.

silver sardines

roast chicken

salty butter

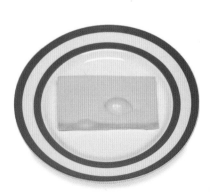

holey cheese

creamy milk

I am drinking cold milk.

In the freezer

Some foods have to be kept frozen.

fish fingers

chunky ice shapes

orange ice lollies

tiny green peas

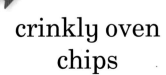

crinkly oven chips

Fruit and vegetables

Do you know what these fruits and vegetables are called?

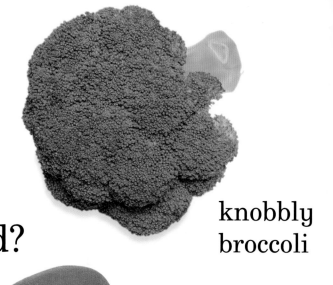

knobbly broccoli

hairy kiwi fruit

sour grapefruit

smooth onions

sweet black grapes

yellow bananas

small potatoes

crisp courgettes

juicy
oranges

crunchy apples

Which fruit shall I have?

Machines and gadgets

The kitchen is full of things to help you do a job more easily.

plastic colander

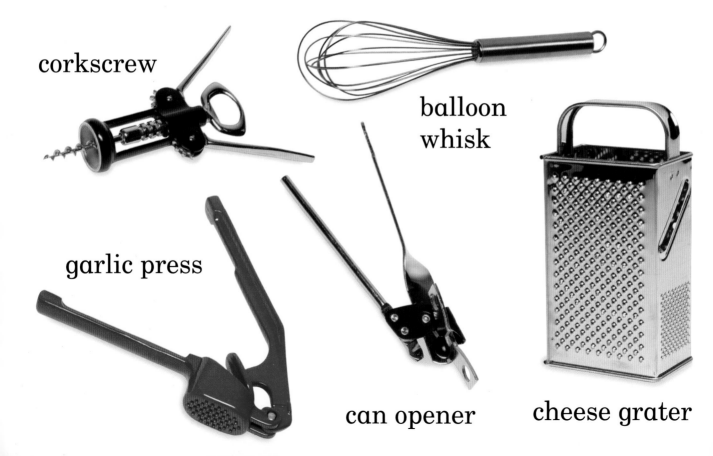

corkscrew

balloon whisk

garlic press

can opener

cheese grater

potato masher

pepper mill

potato peeler

I'm making pancakes for tea.

electric blender

salt mill

Let's cook!

There are lots of special things to cook with in the kitchen.

wooden spoons

oven glove

wire cake rack

casserole dish

frying pan

fish slice

saucepan

slotted
spoon

soup
ladle

cake
tins

Mmm, delicious!

What's for tea?

We often eat our meals in the kitchen.

I'm laying the table.

place mats

forks

teaspoons

knives

dessert spoons

napkins

orange juice

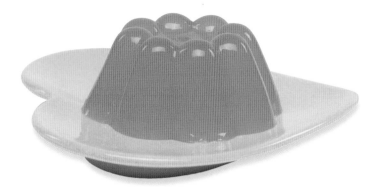

wibbly wobbly jelly

spicy
tomato
pasta

plastic beakers

It's fun to
have a
friend
to tea.

Cleaning up

There are lots of things to help us clean up in the kitchen.

fluffy feather duster

bucket

Almost finished!

sponge

mop

pan scourer

washing-up bowl

dishcloth

washing-up liquid

dustpan and brush

washing-up brush

tea towel

I like mopping the floor best!

bristly broom

What is it for?

Do you know what these kitchen things are for?